A Doctor in the House

By Linda Shenton Matchett

Dedicated to the ordinary women
who did extraordinary things on
the front lines and the Home Front of WWII.

Chapter One

Emma O'Sullivan hurled herself on the floor of the train compartment and covered her head as the shrieking whistle of the approaching bomb filled her ears. Sweat beaded on her upper lip. She cringed and pushed herself further underneath the seat.

Her first mission to England, and she was going to die? The Army Medical Corps hadn't wanted to send her overseas, but she was their last resort to set up the new convalescent hospital. Who would do the work if she was killed?

Time seemed to stand still as the screeching drew closer. A baby cried out, and its mother sobbed in response. Emma squeezed her eyes closed and held her breath. *Is this how You're going to take me home, Lord? Make sure Mom and Dad know I love them.*

A muffled explosion sounded, and the car jolted and bucked its way off the track. Windows shattered, and glass fragments shot through the air. Passengers screamed, and the infant began to wail. Emma shuddered and fought the urge to cry. The little one wasn't the only person frightened. Two days in England, and Emma experienced the trauma many

Londoners had endured for months - unavoidable bombing. Maybe she should have stayed in Baltimore instead of insisting she could handle the assignment. How had she put it? *With one arm tied behind my back.* That might happen after all.

Gray smoke rolled through the jagged openings and filled the train car. Emma climbed to her feet and coughed. Her eyes burned as she surveyed her fellow passengers. "Is anyone hurt? I'm a doctor."

"Over here. It's my mother, she banged her head--"

"I'm bleeding--"

Emma searched for her black leather bag. Dropping to her hands and knees, she rummaged under the paraphernalia that had fallen from the overhead racks. She shoved aside each item and finally found her satchel buried beneath a battered carpet-bag and a pristine Louis Vuitton suitcase.

After crawling to the closest victim, she opened her medical kit. Would she have enough supplies to handle all the wounded? *Lord, help me.*

Blood flowed from a gash on the young woman's arm. Emma patted her shoulder. "I'm Dr. O'Sullivan. I'll fix you up, right as rain. What's your name?"

"Uh…Maggie Burns." She raised tear-filled eyes to Emma's face. "Will there be a scar, miss…I mean, doctor?"

"The cut is long, but doesn't look very deep. I'll do my best." Emma unscrewed a bottle of hydrogen peroxide. "This will hurt a bit, but it's necessary to prevent infection."

Nodding, Maggie pressed her lips together and whimpered quietly when Emma splashed some of the liquid over the laceration before swabbing the area with Dakin's Solution. She pressed a sterile bandage over it and raised the arm to see if any blood soaked through the gauze. When none appeared, she wrapped the arm with a strip of linen and tied it off.

"You're being very brave." Emma smiled and brushed a stray blonde strand away from Maggie's face. "When you get to your destination, you should change the dressing periodically."

After settling Maggie next to an elderly woman who assured her she'd take care of the girl, Emma made her way through the car examining each person. The smoke dissipated as she worked. When she reached the back of the car, she sighed. Her skirt was smudged with rust-colored bloodstains, and her uniform jacket had a tear on one side. Two of the four brass buttons were missing, and a third dangled by a thread. She certainly wouldn't pass inspection in this state.

Touching her head, she grimaced. Her hat was long gone, lost in the blast. The pins had fallen out of her regulation bun, and her hair tumbled down her back. She finger-combed the tresses then tucked them behind her ears. That would have to do for now. Surely there were more wounded in the other cars.

She peeked inside her bag. Good. A decent amount of bandages, sulfa, and other supplies were still nestled in the bottom. Emma climbed out of the train and gasped. Slate-colored smoke billowed toward the overcast sky filled with angry, black clouds. Wreckage was strewn up the hill and down into the ravine. The passenger cars zig-zagged along the track like a giant game of dominoes. Men, women, and children dotted the landscape. Some sat in dazed confusion, others seemed to wander with no purpose, and a few took charge and created order out of chaos.

Squaring her shoulders, Emma set off toward the nearest car. It straddled the railroad ties and listed at a thirty-degree angle. Careful of the glass shards and twisted metal, she hiked across the uneven ground, her two-inch pumps sinking into the grass. When would the Army devise a woman's uniform that was actually practical?

The bottom step was missing, so she grabbed the handrail and tried to hoist herself to the next tread. Her narrow skirt trapped her legs, and she grimaced. Glancing right and left, she confirmed no one seemed to be watching her, so she tugged the garment above her knees and pulled herself inside the train nearly losing a shoe in the process. Despite the chill in the air, perspiration broke out along her hairline.

Her gaze searched the dim interior. At the far end of the car a large, bearded man moved among the dozen or so passengers. His white shirt was torn in several places, and blood saturated his right sleeve. Gray tweed slacks that looked as if they were hand-tailored to fit were rumpled, and his highly-polished, black wingtips bore scuffs and gouges. Smudges of dirt on his swarthy face gave him an air of piracy. He knelt and examined the cut on a small boy.

There were other people to tend to, but the man seemed to be losing blood at an alarming rate. She threaded her way to his side and held up her bag. "Sir, it appears you may need stitching. I've got supplies here and could do that for you."

He swung in her direction, and the gaze from his cobalt-blue eyes pierced her face. His forehead wrinkled, and his mouth was a thin slash. "I'm fine. I don't need some nurse practicing her sewing skills on me. There are others more seriously wounded. See if you can do anything for them."

She faltered. Why did every man she met assume she was a nurse? Not that there was anything wrong with nursing, but she was a full-fledged doctor and had the credentials to prove it. Graduating almost at the top of her class at Johns Hopkins Medical School had proved her detractors wrong.

"Sir, your arm needs to be tended to, and I'm quite capable--"

Looking her up and down, he sneered. "An American, are you? Listen, girlie, I don't take orders from a woman, even if she is wearing a uniform." He shook his head. "What was Roosevelt thinking when he agreed to allow you women in his Army and Navy?"

"He was thinking we could get the job done." She stamped her foot and reached for his sleeve.

Batting her hand away, he rose to his full height. "Let me make myself clear. Push off and go do your nursing in another car. I do not need some upstart, Johnny-come-lately American girl to treat me or my fellow passengers." He turned away and bent over an elderly man who held a scrap of blood-stained cloth against his forehead.

Emma pressed her lips together. Fine. Mr. Upper Crust was on his own. If he bled to death, it'd be his own fault. With any luck, the rest of England's men wouldn't be as infuriating. But without a doubt, few would be as good-looking.

Chapter Two

"Will that be all, sir?"

Archie Heron turned from the window and nodded to his manservant. "Yes, Heath. Have one of the lads take the suitcases to Sparrow Cottage. I'll head down later today."

"Very good, sir. I'll leave you to it." He closed the door with a discreet thump.

Archie pivoted on his heel to gaze outside again. Puffy, white clouds drifted overhead. Surrounded by walled gardens, the manicured lawn was still a vibrant green despite the cool autumn temperatures. The few staff who were too young or too old to enlist or be drafted worked like yeoman to keep the grounds in pre-war condition. How long could that last?

The sound of rumbling engines and squealing brakes filled the air. Archie lifted his eyes toward the meandering driveway. Like a line of lumbering elephants, olive-green, panel trucks marked with red crosses, jeeps, staff cars, and canvas-covered lorries rolled up the macadam path toward the house.

"And so it begins." Archie sighed. The requisition order had arrived only three days ago. Not much time to uproot oneself for the unforeseeable future. A guest on his own property. How would that play out? It was bad enough to lose the house to the war, but did it have to go to the Americans?

Rubbing the back of his neck, he shrugged. As Mum used to say, 'no use crying over spilt milk'. He swallowed against the lump in his throat. Only two years since she died in the Blitz. A bit longer for his brothers thanks to Dunkirk and Trondheim, and his wife, Irene, killed in a bombing raid while visiting Brighton. Dad had been gone since shortly after The Great War. The vicar claimed God had his inscrutable reasons that were for the best. What sort of God wiped out almost an entire family?

Archie blinked away the unbidden tears and took a deep breath. It wouldn't help the situation to get maudlin. Stiff upper lip and all that. He smirked. Wasn't he full of clichés today?

Leaving the window, he moved to the armoire and pulled out the lone suit jacket. He donned the charcoal-colored garment and grimaced when the fabric pulled against the bandage on his arm. He'd be lucky if the gash didn't leave a scar. It had taken hours to see to all the injured after the bombing, so his wound had gone untreated. The doctor who stitched it had lectured him on the dangers of infection.

Perhaps he should have taken his chances with the attractive nurse who had barreled onto the train and insisted she could help. Her golden-green eyes had practically shot flames, and her porcelain skin had darkened when he rebuffed her. She apparently wasn't used to being crossed.

Shaking his head, he took a final look around his boyhood bedroom. Although he was now lord of the manor, there had been no reason to change his sleeping arrangements and move into his parents' room.

Could the Americans appreciate the historicity of the house, or would they simply tromp in and out of the rooms oblivious to the carved fireplaces, gleaming mahogany staircases, flocked wallpaper, and Louis XIV furniture? The housekeeper, Mrs. Eaton, ensured every surface shone with dust-free perfection.

Best to get on with it. He clomped down the stairs and wended his way through the house. Reaching the front entrance, he pressed himself against the wall. Uniformed medics rushed past with crates of supplies, cots, shelving, and evil-looking medical equipment. Their voices bounced and echoed throughout the manor as they shouted to one another.

He slipped outside and jumped back as an ambulance whizzed by then screeched to a halt, its front bumper pushing over the bronze sculpture of a heron that had welcomed guests since Thomas Banks created it in the mid-1700s. The statue hit the ground with a clank, and the driver hopped out of the vehicle, eyes wide and panic-stricken.

"Golly, I didn't mean to knock over your bird. What's he doing in the driveway? Think you could give me a hand in setting the poor thing upright?" The sandy-haired young man whose freckled, clean-shaven face didn't look more than eighteen ducked his head and blushed.

Archie gritted his teeth and glowered. "Watch where you're going. How did you manage to get this truck to Heron Hall without crashing?"

"I'm sorry, sir. I guess I misjudged the distance. Is the bird very important?"

"Other than being my personal property, yes, the statue is important. But I would think you'd try not to hit it just on principle. Hmmm?"

"No, sir…I mean yes, sir."

"Which is it?" Archie towered over the medic. "It's bad enough my home is being overrun by a bunch of Americans without so much as a by-your-leave, but do you have to begin demolishing the property as soon as you arrive? What sort of operation is this? Who's in charge here?"

"Uh, Major O'Sullivan. The doctor should be here any minute. You can address your…uh…concerns with her."

"Her?" Archie's lip curled. The Americans had a *woman* heading up this hospital? If she was anything like the pushy nurse on the train, he was done for.

He shook his head as a staff car rolled to a stop in front of him. The driver climbed out and rushed to open the back door. A ginger-headed woman wearing a brown, officer's uniform stepped out and looked up. She met his eyes, and her mouth formed a perfect O as she gaped at him.

Staring, Archie took a step forward. "What are you doing here? You're a doctor? You said you were a nurse."

Her eyes flashed, and she emitted a harsh laugh. "No, *you* said I was a nurse. I could barely get a word in edgewise as you hurled assumptions at me." She held up the Notice of Requisition of Premises. "I'm afraid your worst nightmares have come true. Not only am I a doctor, but as Hospital Administrator, I'm in charge here. Now, we have a lot of work to do before the first patients arrive, so as much as I'm enjoying this little sparring match, I must leave you." She handed the notice to the driver. "Sergeant, if you wouldn't mind."

"Yes, ma'am." He walked to the front entrance and slapped the paper onto a nail protruding from the stone edifice then arranged himself at attention next to the door.

The woman dipped her head in dismissal. "Please excuse me." With ramrod precision, she marched into the house and disappeared from view.

Archie finger-combed his hair then scrubbed at his face with cold hands. This was a disaster in the making. He'd find out who her superior officer was and get her transferred. Surely there was someone else better suited to the job. No one that young or that prickly could manage a military convalescent hospital. She needed to return to America, and he was just the person to make that happen.

Chapter Three

Emma pressed her lips together and stalked through the house. Her heels banged out a staccato rhythm on the wood floors. Thumps, bumps, and clangs ricocheted into the corridor, and voices populated every corner of the building. A line of cots was already growing in the ballroom. Perhaps the hospital would be ready on time in spite of the owner's efforts to have her booted out.

Her face heated. How dare he threaten her? She was here on behalf of the American Army, for goodness sake. Didn't he understand she was on his side? He obviously didn't care. Or maybe he was so angry at having to give up his estate he was taking out his bad mood on everyone.

She entered the dining room and froze. The ceiling rose at least twenty-five feet over her head and was painted with several familial scenes. One wall was completely windowed and looked out over a massive formal garden. The other walls were covered with a burgundy and gold flocked paper. A gleaming, cherry table stretched long enough to easily seat thirty or more patients. If she moved it from the center of the room, she could bring in additional tables.

The sideboard held an ornate silver tea set guarded by a portrait of a stern-looking man reminiscent of her cranky host. No doubt one of his relatives. Judging by the subject's clothing, the painting must be close to four hundred years old. What was it like to be part of that much history? She barely knew her second cousins and had never known her mother's parents who had died when Mom was a child.

No wonder their host was skittish about turning his place into an Army hospital. He probably figured it wouldn't survive the occupation. Emma shrugged. With the amount of money he must have as a duke, earl or whatever he was, surely he could repair any damage that occurred. She cocked her head. What *was* his name? She was so surprised to see him, and then he had nearly bitten off her head. She had to escape into the house before introductions could be made.

Movement outside the window caught her attention, and she inched closer for a better look. "Speaking of His Highness, there he is now." She covered her mouth and watched as he sauntered along the stone path circling the flower beds. Hands stuffed into his pockets, he walked with his head down and shoulders bowed. The breeze ruffled his thick, dark hair and the blue muffler wrapped around his neck.

The man seated himself on a stone bench under an elm tree then looked up and met her eyes through the window. With a sardonic grin, he put his hand to his forehead in a mock salute. She gasped and stepped back. Of all the arrogance! And she had begun to feel sorry for him. Well, that stopped here and now. She had a job to do, and he needed to stay out of her way.

Footsteps sounded behind Emma. A diminutive woman dressed in a nurse's uniform stood in the doorway. A white cap perched on top of her blonde curls. "Dr. O'Sullivan?"

"Yes."

"I'm Gwen Milford, head nurse assigned to the hospital. I thought we could tour the house and discuss how to best use the space. The men have begun to set up the ballroom and four of the largest parlors as wards, but we'll need to determine offices, exam, and treatment rooms as well as recreational space." Her voice held a slight southern drawl. "This is about the biggest house I've ever seen. My parent's home would fit inside this room."

Emma smiled. "It is a monstrosity, but that means we should have plenty of room to carry out our orders. If the first floor is an indicator of the rest of the manor, we have our work cut out for us. The hallways and most of the doorways don't seem wide enough for the gurneys, and there are stairs everywhere. Several of the rooms have rugs which will need to be removed-they're a breeding ground for germs. The lighting leaves much to be desired also, but there are lots of large windows which should help."

"Fortunately, it has been fitted with indoor plumbing. My last assignment was at an evac hospital located two miles from the front with tents and privies." Gwen shuddered. "Anything is better than that." Her face brightened. "Have you seen the guy who owns the place? He's a real looker in a brooding, Heathcliff sort of way. Sir Archibald Heron. Archie to his friends. His family was granted the land by royal charter almost five hundred years ago. Not too shabby, huh?"

"We've met, and he's made it plain that he's not happy I'm here."

"What's his complaint? The fact that you're an American? Some of the British don't seem to appreciate our presence."

"That and my being a female doctor. He didn't seem to quite believe my credentials."

"How Victorian of him." Gwen winked. "Well, he's been relegated to one of the guest houses, so with any luck he'll stay out of our way. Although, I wouldn't mind a peek at him time and again. He's a handsome one."

"I think you're going to see him plenty. He claims he's going to do his best to have me replaced."

Gwen gave a dismissive wave. "Let him try. Meanwhile, let's see what we can do about this mansion of his."

Emma squared her shoulders and exited the room. What had she gotten herself into?

Chapter Four

Archie tossed his pen on the desk and closed the ledger. Pushing the book away, he rose and rubbed his burning eyes. A month had passed since the requisition, and he was no closer to having the American interloper transferred. She still ruled over the hospital with tenacity and a firm hand.

He massaged the stiffness from his shoulder where a bullet had struck him during the Battle of France. Patched up and returned to combat, he continued to serve until his brothers' deaths. Because he was the sole surviving male in the family, the British Army discharged him. As brutal as the fighting had been, he had loved the challenge of executing the strategies of his superior officers. People had looked up to him and followed his leadership. Being the youngest of three sons, he had never experienced that.

"And now I'm commanding a Home Guard unit filled with old men and lads too young to enlist." Sighing, he began to pace. "How the mighty have fallen."

A discreet knock sounded at the door, and Heath entered the room carrying a tray. A blue, Wedgewood teapot and a lone teacup sat next to a plate piled with finger sandwiches. Creative even before the war, Mrs.

Eaton worked miracles providing sustenance on rations.

"Set it on the desk, Heath."

"Thank you, sir."

"A little beneath you to be serving tea, isn't it?"

Heath shrugged.

Archie narrowed his eyes. "Perhaps there's something you'd like to tell me?"

"If I may be so bold, sir, you shouldn't stay cooped up in the cottage. You haven't been outside in days, and it's a lovely day for a stroll in the gardens. Unseasonably warm, it is."

"Trying to get me out from underfoot, are you?"

Heath's face reddened to the roots of his hair. "No, sir. Just trying to look after you."

"May I have my tea first, or would you like me to leave immediately?"

"Of course you may have your tea--"

"Relax, Heath, I'm teasing. You're right. A walk around the property is long overdue, and I'll get to it straightaway." Archie grinned. "Would you like to come with me?"

"That wouldn't be proper, sir, and I've much to do here in the house."

"Heath, we've known each other since we were both in nappies. Your father served my father. Can't we set aside this class nonsense for once?"

A frown wrinkled Heath's forehead. "What would the other staff say? It could cause dissension in the ranks, if you look like you're playing favorites."

"Forget I asked. I don't want to cause problems for you."

"Thank you, sir." Heath bowed slightly then hurried from the room.

Archie sighed. His head understood protocol, but his heart ached with loneliness. His mates were either dead or somewhere overseas. Sometimes it would be nice to debate ideas over a pint, or play chess in front of the fire.

His gaze strayed to the teapot. "Grandmother, what would you make of the war?" Walking to the desk, he poured himself a cup and quickly downed the flavorful, amber liquid. No need to dawdle. Sunshine beckoned. He strode from the office and out of the house.

Warmth caressed his face as he stepped outside. Blowing out a deep breath, Archie smiled. Heath was right; he had been inside too long. He set off across the lawn, arms swinging and his feet sinking into the spongy cushion of grass. Reaching the brick path, he sauntered toward the small pond at the edge of the woods. The last of the wildflowers dipped and bobbed their heads. A hawk soared on the thermals above, the bird's intermittent shrieks cutting through the air.

Archie hummed under his breath. He shielded his eyes against the sun's glare and gazed across the undulating meadows of the estate. Continuing along the walkway, he arrived at the water and sat on the banks. A pair of geese swam and fed in the center of the pond. The war seemed far away. *Thank You, God, for Your lovely creation and providing for my needs. I don't deserve Your goodness.*

The crack of gunshot echoed behind him, and he leapt to his feet.

A second shot sounded. Whipping his head back and forth, Archie tried to determine where the noise had come from. The woods? The house? Had some patient gone mad? Setting off at a run, he sped toward the manor. Breathless, he approached the gothic Tudor. The driveway and grounds were vacant. Was everyone inside? Were they being held hostage?

Heart pounding, he raced into the house. Dr. O'Sullivan and the matron stood to one side of the foyer, deep in conversation. Archie came to an abrupt stop. "Did you not hear that?"

The two women turned toward him and shook their heads. "Hear what?" Dr. O'Sullivan asked.

"The gunshots. I was at the far end of the property and heard the reports. I thought they came from here." He cocked his head. "You didn't hear anything?"

"I'm afraid not. Perhaps you were imagining things."

"I'm not one of your patients who has lost his faculties, *Doctor.*" Archie spoke through gritted teeth. "I know what I heard. But if everything is in order here, I'll be on my way."

"We're fine. We appreciate your concern." Her tone suggested anything but appreciation.

Huffing a breath, Archie turned and stalked from the house. He marched to the driveway and stopped. Speechless, he stared across the meadow. Coming out of the woods and making their way across the grassy expanse was a pair of orderlies. Trussed up on a pole and slung between them was a young male, red deer. One of *his* red deer.

Chapter Five

Pushing the food around on her plate, Emma sagged against the back of her chair. The cook had created a tantalizing meal from yesterday's ill-gotten venison, but Emma had little appetite for the aromatic, succulent meat. After last night's thirty-minute tirade denigrating her skills as a doctor, an administrator, and a person in general, Sir Heron had threatened to contact the Minister of Food about the deer, claiming her career would cease to exist once he reported the incident.

She shook her head at the look of triumph on his face as he made the proclamation. Did he despise her that much? They had barely spoken during the month since the hospital's inception, yet he seemed to hold her in total contempt. As far as she could tell, the men had done nothing wrong in taking down the stag. Hunting season lasted from August to April for male red deer.

Her gaze swept the room, and she smiled at the enthusiasm of the patients. Forks and knives eagerly scraped against the china plates as the men devoured their dinner. Fortunately, the facility was not at full capacity yet, so each person received a good sized portion.

Leaning toward Gwen, Emma gestured to her plate. "We're going to have to see about reimbursing Sir Heron for his venison. How can I find out what I should pay him?"

"He insists the men call him Archie. You should, too."

"No." Her face warmed. "It's best if we keep things on a professional level and using his first name won't do that."

"Are you blushing?" Gwen giggled. "I don't blame you. You already know I think he's the tops."

"You're getting off topic."

A mischievous smiled played on Gwen's lips. "I'd much rather discuss our gorgeous host than our dinner."

"That's obvious, but I'm serious. Perhaps if I make reparations, he won't notify the authorities." Emma blew out a breath. "This assignment means everything to me. I can't lose it."

Gwen straightened. "All right. I'll see if one of the orderlies can make some discreet inquiries. Procurement might be able to help."

"I don't want to go through official channels if I don't have to. I'd like to stay out of the limelight, if possible."

"You're doing a wonderful job, Dr. O'Sullivan. I've worked under several doctors, and you're one of the best I've seen. You need to relax. You work much too hard. Perhaps if you spent time getting to know Sir Archie…"

"Stop. It's not going to happen. He hates me."

Gwen took a sip of tea then dabbed her mouth with the napkin. "The lady doth protest too much, methinks."

"You're using Shakespeare to make your point?" Emma laid her fork on the plate. "Listen, even if I was *theoretically* attracted to Sir Archie, he made it clear from the get-go he dislikes Americans, women, and doctors. And since I'm all three, he must have a three-fold dislike of me. Why open myself up to rejection? I had enough of that trying to prove myself in med school. Let's face it, that man can't handle a woman who is in charge. You can have him."

"I'm not on the market. I already have a beau, and if we both survive this war, we're going to get married."

"Well, I'm not on the market either. I have a career I love, and I don't need a man, especially one as cranky as Sir Archie, no matter how good-looking he is."

Chortling, Gwen clapped her hands. "Aha! I knew you thought he was handsome. That thick, wavy hair and close-cropped beard. And his eyes..." She fanned herself. "I could lose myself in those crystal blue eyes. I'll bet they sparkle like fire, and his whole face lights up when he laughs."

"Seeing as how that isn't going to happen, we'll never know."

"Pshaw. I think there's hope for him. He's had a difficult life. I was talking to one of the medics who said Archie lost his whole family, including his wife, in the war. That has to do something to a person. Maybe he's not cross, but rather overwhelmed with grief." She wiped a stray tear from her face. "And you're just the person to help him."

Emma patted Gwen's shoulder. "You're such a softie. Do you

think if I keep up our feud that will heal him?" She shook her head. "You have a strange way of looking at life."

"Go out of your way to be nice to him." Gwen looked over her glasses at Emma. "*Pray* for him."

Chest tightening, Emma winced. "You're right. I've been so upset about what happened after the train was bombed on the day we arrived, I haven't given him the benefit of the doubt. I just assumed he was a crotchety, ill-mannered Englishman and have been treating him as such. No wonder he's been churlish."

"So we have a deal? You'll start praying for him *and* being nice to him?"

Emma crossed her arms and nibbled on her lower lip. "I don't have to like it, do I?"

Gwen burst out laughing. "No, but I think you do."

Waving away the comment, Emma said, "Shows what you know." Then why did her stomach quiver as if a flock of hummingbirds had taken flight inside? Why did she care what he thought of her? Whatever the reason, the truth was that she did care.

But she'd do everything in her power to ensure he never knew his belittling her efforts hurt.

Chapter Six

Archie stepped into Sparrow Cottage and shed his Home Guard jacket. He started to toss the garment on the coat rack then changed his mind and carried it upstairs and hung it in the bedroom closet. Heath and Mrs. Eaton had enough to do without having to pick up after him. He changed into a pair of worn, brown corduroy pants and pulled a tan cardigan over his shirt.

Drilling the Home Guard troops had filled most of the morning. The men took pride in their unit and insisted on practicing until they mastered their moves. Today had been spent on weapons handling and unarmed combat, and with the exception of one man's broken nose, drills had gone well. Ragged from calling out instructions, his throat was parched. A cup of tea and a good book were in order.

Stomach rumbling, Archie trotted down the stairs and into the small kitchen. He opened the fridge and smiled. Mrs. Eaton had prepared several egg and watercress sandwiches. What would he do without her?

He seated himself at the small wooden table and bowed his head. *Lord, thank You for this food and Mrs. Eaton who prepared it. Let me never take her for granted. Bless her today as she serves the staff at the manor. In Your Son's name, amen.*

Taking a bite, he moaned. The eggs had been cooked to perfection, and the sharp, pepper-like flavor of the watercress warmed his tongue. Did the hospital staff appreciate Mrs. Eaton's abilities? Did Dr. O'Sullivan realize what she had in his unassuming housekeeper?

"Probably not. She's too young and too stubborn." His stomach cramped, and he laid the sandwich on his plate. He was being unfair. In the two weeks since the debacle about the deer, she had been pleasant, even solicitous whenever they chanced to meet. And three days ago, Heath informed him she had reimbursed the household account for the cost of the animal. Apparently unhappy with the sloth-like pace of the Ministry of Food, she had paid the money from her own pocket.

"She's got integrity. I'll give her that." Picking up the bread, he finished the meal. Why did she have to be a redhead? He had a weakness for ginger-haired women. Strawberry-colored strands glimmered and shone as they escaped the tight bun she wore at the nape of her neck. He had only seen her once in street clothes, something he'd never forget. Her hair was drawn up on the sides with two combs, and the rest tumbled below her shoulders in glistening waves. Dressed in a slim, navy blue skirt and light blue sweater, she was the picture of prim and proper. Yet, the simplicity of her outfit drew him as if she were adorned for an evening of dinner and dancing.

She wore a small, garnet ring on her right hand, but her left hand was ringless. Was she walking out with anyone? Did she have a special someone waiting for her at home or was he in uniform somewhere around the globe?

"Get ahold of yourself, old man. You want her off your property, yet here you sit daydreaming about her." Archie stood and washed his plate before returning it to the cupboard. He set the kettle on to boil, and stared out the window over the sink while he waited.

A muted knock sounded behind him.

Heath stood in the doorway. "There is a General Winn here to see you. He's…ah…from the Americans. I took the liberty of ushering him into the east parlor. What shall I tell him, sir?"

"Did he say what he wants?"

"No, but he does seem to be in a bit of a rush, so perhaps he won't take up too much of your time."

"Time isn't the issue, but rather why I have yet another American Army officer on site." Archie shrugged. "Head back to the main house. I'll see him straightaway."

"Yes, sir." Heath pivoted on his heel and disappeared, his footsteps fading.

Archie turned off the gas and strode to the parlor. So much for a book and a cuppa. Graham Greene's latest novel would have to wait.

Forking his fingers through his hair, Archie squared his shoulders and entered the room. Extending his hand to the portly, balding man, he smiled. "Archibald Heron."

"General James Winn. A pleasure to meet you."

Gesturing to one of the Queen Anne chairs near the fireplace,

Archie seated himself in its twin. "How can I help you, General?"

Winn steepled his fingers and looked at Archie from hooded eyes. "I'm here in response to your request to have Dr. O'Sullivan reassigned elsewhere. I understand there have been, how shall we say it, *incidents* that may warrant our attention. Do you have specifics to back up your claims of incompetence?"

Archie straightened. They sent a general to handle his complaint. Did the man have nothing better to do? How would his involvement affect the doctor's career? Swallowing, he rubbed the back of his neck.

"Well, speak up. I've traveled some distance to meet with you, and I need to get back to the war."

Did the man's arrogance know no bounds?

"Of course. Thank you for coming. I'll get right to it. Two of her staff killed a red deer stag from my herd. It was butchered and used to feed the patients, but they had no right to hunt on private property. The other situation is her management of the hospital in general. The patients are not required to wear their hospital uniforms and are seen around the property in all manner of dress. And she has set up a performance hall." Archie frowned. "These men need rest and care, not vaudeville and games."

"I understand your concerns and am in complete agreement. With regard to the buck, Dr. O'Sullivan will receive a formal reprimand, and you may seek compensation from the American War Department or your own Ministry of Food. Either way, I'm betting it will be a while before you see any money." He pursed his lips. "As far as getting the good doctor out of your house, it's not going to happen, at least not yet. Because of the number of battle locations, the Army Medical Corps has a shortage of qualified physicians to run the convalescent hospitals. And with Roosevelt's latest mandate, we've got to keep the women, including Dr. O'Sullivan, in place for the time being."

"Even if the woman isn't up to scratch?"

Winn put on his hat and stood. "I'll admit her methods are a bit unorthodox, and I'm not happy about women in the ranks, but her recovery rates are among the highest in the Corps. Send your proof to me at the SHAEF headquarters in London. For now, she stays." He dipped his head in a curt nod. "I'll see myself out."

Unorthodox? More like barking mad. He'd have to spend more time at the manor to collect the necessary evidence about the doctor's performance. Snapping his fingers, he grinned. The head nurse was overly friendly, flirtatious even. He could use that to his advantage. Then it wouldn't be long before a certain doctor found herself back in America.

Chapter Seven

Standing on a chair in the east parlor, Emma held a wreath of red poppies against the wall. She spoke through the nail clenched between her teeth. "Is it high enough?"

Gwen pointed to the right. "Yes, but move it over a tad; it's not quite centered."

Juggling the floral circlet and the hammer, Emma tapped the nail into the wood paneling, then hung the flowers.

"Perfect." The head nurse peeked into the box of boutonnieres. "It was very generous of Archie to secure flowers for the boys. He's a fascinating man, don't you think?"

"If you call criticizing me at every opportunity and attempting to have me transferred fascinating. But I agreed to be nice and pray for him, so that's what I'm doing." Emma shrugged as she jumped off the chair and then tucked the tool into the small desk in the corner of the room.

"He'll come around, you'll see."

"Maybe. Meanwhile, I'll do what the Army has commanded me to do." She glanced at the clock, and her mouth dried out. Nearly an hour before the remembrance ceremony began and Sir Heron's arrival. The commemoration would be short - two minutes of silence in memory of those who had fallen during The Great War followed by a prayer and brief homily by the chaplain. She licked her lips. Any time in their host's presence was excruciating. *Lord, help me be polite. Don't let my mouth run away with my face.*

"You're a stubborn one, I'll give you that." Gwen held up a poppy. "I was eight when the war ended. How about you?"

Emma blinked. "Uh, seven. My mother took me to the celebration in our town. Bells in every church rang, and there were thousands of people in the streets. Very exciting for a little girl. My dad came home a few months later, but one of his brothers was killed between the armistice and the ceasefire."

"How tragic."

"Yeah, Dad doesn't talk much about his time away." Emma frowned. "Did your dad serve?"

"Yes, but we were lucky. He worked for one of the aircraft manufacturers. Sometimes I think he was embarrassed about not being called up."

"That's too bad. Men were needed to produce materiel. It was an important job."

"Now they've got us women helping out."

"Women volunteered and took jobs during the last war, but not as many as this go-round." Emma crossed her arms. "Do you think the King will attend the ceremony at the Cenotaph?"

"I would think so. He and the Queen seem intent on keeping up appearances. Did you know Buckingham Palace was bombed back in '40 and again in '41, yet they insist on remaining in residence? The English are a brave lot. I'm proud to serve here."

"Me, too." Emma fingered the blooms in the box. "I hope the observance doesn't upset the boys. They're discouraged enough about being wounded. Perhaps we should consider some sort of entertainment tomorrow or Tuesday as a pick-me-up."

"Great idea. I'll speak with Lisa and Polly. They love arranging that sort of thing." Gwen's brow wrinkled. "Why do you think God allowed Hitler to gain power and cause this awful war?"

Emma rubbed her temples. "I've wondered that myself countless times, but evil is part of our fallen world. Terrible leaders will do horrific things. We'll probably never know why God lets wars happen."

"So many innocent people have died, and who knows how many more before it's over." A tear trickled down Gwen's cheek, and she swiped it away. "Sorry for getting weepy--must be all the poppies. Let's think on happier things, like what we're going to do after the war."

"You're going to settle down with a swell, young man and have lots of beautiful babies who look just like you. And you're such a softie; you'll probably take in lots of stray cats and dogs, too. How does that sound?"

Gwen giggled. "Exhausting. I like the part about the guy, but I'm not sure about all those kids and animals."

"Really? You'd be a wonderful mom. I see how nurturing you are with the patients."

"Enough about me. I think all this praying is going to cause you to fall madly in love with our Archie, and you'll stay here as baroness or duchess or whatever you're supposed to be called as wife of the Lord of the manor. You'll use your influence and do great things, my Lady. " She dipped in a graceful curtsy. "How does that sound?"

"Like a nightmare. First of all, I want to stay in medicine, and no man is going to let me do that, so marriage isn't in the cards for this girl. Secondly, I'm never going to fall in love with "our Archie," as you put it." She shuddered. "And I'm certainly not going to stay in this soggy, drafty country where rules are rules and the class system is alive and well."

Emma bit her lip. Why did the thought of going home make her stomach flop?

Chapter Eight

The wind whistled and nipped at Archie's face as he approached the manor. He hunched further into his wool jacket before stepping inside the house. It was on days like this he regretted the lack of central heating in the house, but the cost of installation was exorbitant, and by summer, the expenditure seemed frivolous. Emma made it clear she was not happy with the situation, claiming the chill impacted the patients' healing. Was that true or was it her thin American blood that couldn't stand the temperature?

Checking his appearance in the mirror above the table in the entryway, he shook his head. It didn't matter what he looked like. The wounded certainly wouldn't care. In fact, they would probably prefer to be visited by one of the nurses or the dishy doctor herself.

He froze and stared at his reflection. Whoa. When had he started thinking of Emma as attractive? Or just plain Emma instead of Doctor O'Sullivan? Archie rubbed his forehead and strode through the corridor. *Focus, man. You've got to stay on task. Just because the doctor is a beautiful woman doesn't mean she should be running a hospital.*

His attempt to engage Sister Milford-or Head Nurse Milford as the Americans would say- in his plan to discredit Emma had met with little success. Despite the way the nurse flirted in his vicinity, smiling and winking, the woman's loyalty to Emma appeared unswerving. Regularly commenting about Emma's abilities and treatment of the patients, the nurse seemed to go out of her way to give him her high opinion of the facility and its administrator. There had to be another way to collect the needed evidence.

Archie entered the ballroom-turned-hospital-ward and nodded at the white-clad nurse sitting behind the desk.

She smiled. "Good evening, Sir Heron. The men have been looking forward to your visit. I've scrounged up some paper if you'd like to play tic-tac-toe, or as you English call it, naughts and crosses."

"Thank you, but I thought I'd read to the lads tonight." He pulled a small volume from his pocket. "I got my hands on the latest Agatha Christie. Nothing like a good murder mystery, don't you think?"

"Yes, sir." She poured a glass of water from the pitcher at her elbow and held it out to him. "Can't have you losing your voice before we find out how Miss Marple catches the culprit."

"Quite right." He took the drink and sauntered down the aisle, stopping at each bed to say a few words. These were brave chaps. They knew they would be returned to the front to fight again, yet most of them laughed often and chipped him about his accent or some aspect of life in England.

"Sir Archie, I gotta beef. My beer at dinner was warm."

Archie grinned and wagged his finger at the young man. "Who in their right mind drinks cold beer? Besides, I happen to know the good doctor does not allow spirits in the hospital. The only alcohol you're going to see is what they use to clean your injuries."

A chorus of jeers rose, and he chuckled. They were in rare form tonight. "Anyone else have complaints before we get on with it?" He held up the book.

"Nothing that can't wait." This from a lad with casts on both arms and a bandage over one eye. Archie swallowed past the lump forming in his throat and dragged a chair to the center of the room. "Let's get to it then, shall we?" Seating himself, he opened the novel. *"The Moving Finger* by Agatha Christie...*"

Thirty minutes later Archie closed the book and drained the last of his water. "I'm parched. Does anyone want to take over reading?"

"None of us has your nifty accent. An American reading an English novel doesn't seem right."

"Yeah, come back again tomorrow. It will be like those serials they do on the radio…uh…wireless, only in person."

"Thanks for coming, sir. You're a swell guy for a swanky honcho."

Archie rose and tucked the novel into his pocket. "I hope that's a good thing."

The young man nodded and gave him a thumbs up.

Returning his chair to the corner of the room, Archie waved and turned to leave. Footsteps sounded from the hall, and Emma appeared in the doorway, her arms filled with blankets. Didn't she have more important tasks than delivering bedding? He dipped his head and held out his arms. "May I be of service?"

Their eyes met, and her face pinked. "Thanks, but I'm okay. I'm sure you have better things to do."

"Not at the moment, no."

"Fine." She thrust the pile at him, then turned to the woman behind her. "Are there any more blankets in the storeroom?"

"That's the last of them, ma'am."

"All right, see how far they go." Emma looked at Archie and swiped at a ginger strand that had fallen across her forehead. "Lay one at the foot of each bed. The girls will see about covering the men. Then meet me in my office, we have something we need to discuss."

He stared at her retreating figure until the woman beside him cleared her throat. "Sir? The blankets?"

"Uh, sorry…yes...of course."

Ignoring her knowing smile, he practically sprinted through the ward to drop a blanket at each cot.

Minutes later he rapped on his library-turned-office door frame as he pinned a look of interest on his face.

Emma gestured to the burgundy, Queen Anne chair beside her desk. "Please have a seat."

"You seem out of sorts. Perhaps the job is overwhelming."

She crossed her arms and scowled. "Nice try, Sir Heron. I'm not upset because of my workload. It's this house. We can't keep it warm, and the patients are suffering because of it. You and Nurse Callahan distributed the few remaining blankets we had. The delivery we received yesterday labeled blankets was a crate of mosquito netting. Not exactly helpful. To top things off, we've run out of dry wood for the fireplaces."

"And how does that affect me?"

"Even though the American Army is using Heron Hall, this is your home. I'm trying to be a good steward of the property, but frankly, I'm at my wit's end about heating it. Cutting down your trees won't do any good, because the wood will be too green."

A sour taste filled his mouth. What diabolical plan was she going to propose? "Please get to the point, Doctor."

"Fine. I scoured the house for alternative sources and found quite a few wooden chairs in the basement I'd like to break apart, and I'd like to remove the paneling in the west parlor. I haven't surveyed the property. Do you have any sheds that could be dismantled?"

Archie widened his eyes. *Unorthodox?* General Winn's comment was an understatement. She wanted to desecrate the parlor, destroy his furniture, and decimate the outbuildings. He leapt to his feet and poked his finger at her. "Have you no shame? This home has been in my family for generations, and you show up with your batty schemes to burn it to the ground one piece at a time. Would you like a staircase or two, or perhaps the doors?"

Her face paled, yet she rose to stand ramrod stiff. "Apparently you hold your precious house and its contents more important than the well-being of these courageous boys who fought to keep *your* country safe from Hitler. What was I thinking to ask you for a bit of wood to warm the wards enough to ensure the wounded can heal properly? Your whole I-care-about-the-men-let-me-visit-and-read-to-them act is a sham. They mean bupkis to you. You only think about yourself." Her voice held venom as she fisted her hands.

"In an effort to keep the peace, I sought your permission before I had the orderlies do anything, yet you chew me out as if I've already begun. I've tried to give you the respect your title deserves, and stupid me, I even prayed for you, but I've little use for a man who cares only about his own needs. Get out."

"Rest assured, this ill-mannered tirade will go into my report to General Winn."

She shrugged. "And until he boots me out of here, I'll continue to serve the men. With or without your help."

He strode from the room, heart pounding. Use his chairs as kindling. Outrageous. And she prayed for him. Wait. She prayed for him? He closed his eyes. *Lord, what are You doing? What am I doing?*

Chapter Nine

Emma wiped away the perspiration on her forehead with her sleeve then continued to macerate the massive bowl of steaming potatoes. Gwen pared a mountain of carrots at the other end of the table. A full Thanksgiving dinner for the patients required all hands on deck, even the hospital administrator. Thrusting the masher into the lumpy, white mixture, she grimaced. "At least potatoes don't argue with me at every turn, like a certain pig-headed Englishman."

Her shoulder muscles clenched. It had been a while since she had to do such physical labor. Maybe she should help out in the kitchen more often. There was a certain reward in completing such simple chores. "Wouldn't Sir Difficult be happy to see me relegated to the cookhouse?"

"Is everything all right, Doctor? You're mumbling to the potatoes. " Mrs. Eaton stood at the stove, wooden spoon in hand. She cocked her head. "Are they misbehaving?"

"Uh, I'm fine." Emma grinned. "I'm wrangling the potatoes into submission." She bent over the bowl. Had the housekeeper heard anything incriminating? Did she know how much Emma disliked the woman's boss? Was Mrs. Eaton part of Archie's plan to have Emma transferred?

"Let me know if you tire, and one of the scullery maids can take your place."

"Thank you." *Lord, You know I'm struggling. I thought You called me to serve here in England, but now I'm not sure. Is Sir Heron Your way of telling me I missed what You were saying? Lead me, Father. I want to serve where You want me.* She nibbled her lower lip. *And bless the boys today. Give them Your comfort and peace as they face this holiday injured and far from home.*

A clatter sounded at the door, and it opened with a bang. Two orderlies entered carrying firewood. Sir Heron was close on their heels.

Emma narrowed her eyes. What was the man up to? In the two weeks since their argument, he had made himself scarce. When he did show up, his attitude was distant. Now, he came bearing a few logs like that was going to make a difference.

She gripped the masher and pressed her lips together. *Lord, keep my mouth shut.*

Gwen giggled, and Emma stuck out her tongue at her friend before bending over her work.

"Doctor, where would you like us to put the wood?" Archie's smooth baritone voice washed over her, and her breath quickened. Suddenly he was Archie? Get a grip, Emma.

Attempting to seem impassive, she turned to the men. "On the hearth in the east parlor. Many of the ambulatory patients pass their time there, and it's smaller than the wards, so should stay warm for a while after the wood is gone."

Rudy, the burlier of the two orderlies, jerked his head toward the door. "There's more where this came from, ma'am."

"What?"

He held up the log. "There's a whole passel of wood, Doctor O'Sullivan. Sir Heron…ah…Archie got a bunch delivered. We're going to be warm all the way through the winter. What a guy, huh?" Rudy clomped out of the kitchen followed by the other orderly.

Emma clamped her mouth shut and swung her gaze to Archie, whose face was an uncharacteristic shade of red. Was he actually embarrassed? She crossed her arms and continued to stare at him. "Is this true, Sir Heron? You brought enough wood to heat the house for the entire winter? How did you manage that?"

He set the logs on the floor and brushed off his hands. "Just because I don't want my house dismantled, doesn't mean I want the lads to suffer. I used my contacts to source the firewood. One of my friends has closed up his home and moved to Liverpool. The government hasn't shown an interest in requisitioning his place, so I secured his supply. Another couple of friends are seeking assistance from their associates. I'm optimistic we'll get additional wood."

"Why are you doing this? What do you get out of it?" Emma frowned. "You realize if you help me, it will hinder your case of my incompetence, don't you?"

His face darkened. "You need wood. I found a solution. Why is that so difficult to comprehend?"

"I understand you found a solution. My question is why? There doesn't seem to be anything in it for you, so I'm stunned at your generosity. You haven't exactly been a model of benevolence since our arrival."

He glanced around the room and seemed to take in the audience of nurses and kitchen staff. "Would you please give us a moment?"

The women scurried from the room like mice startled by a hungry cat. The door swung back and forth for a moment before settling to a close.

Leaning against the counter, Archie licked his lips. "Our relationship got off on the wrong foot, and I'm sorry for that. You have a challenging job to do, and I'm making it more difficult. I apologize for my behavior."

Who was this man? "What happened? Did you get a glimpse of your own mortality, or is this a way to lull me into a false sense of security?"

"I beg your pardon?"

"You've been abominable, and then suddenly you show up with a few truckloads of wood and an apology. I want to know why."

He blew out a loud sigh and rubbed the back of his neck before meeting her gaze. "You said you were praying for me. That stopped me in my tracks. I'm sure it will come as a surprise to you that I'm a Christian. Nurse Milford indicated the two of you are as well, and instead of welcoming you as a fellow believer, I've harangued you and tried to subvert you at every turn. Can you forgive me?"

Emma gaped at him for a long moment. He was a Christian? *Is he really, Lord, or is this a trick? He seems to be extending an olive branch, but it could be a poison ivy leaf in disguise. What do I do?*

Archie shrugged and bent to pick up the wood. "I'll take that as a no and won't waste any more of your time. The lorry drivers will stack the bulk of the delivery outside, and I'll ask Rudy and Tony to bring some in for each fireplace." Without a backward glance he pushed through the door with his shoulder and disappeared, his footsteps fading.

Trust him, my child.

"Now You tell me, Lord?" Her heart squeezed. Archie's apology had seemed genuine, his handsome face a combination of guilt and shame. And she had gawked at him like one of the giant sturgeons in the river. She'd find him and set his mind at ease. Her chest lightened, and she shook her head.

"Don't be a ninny, Emma. You've a job to do, and when it's finished you're returning to the States. Archie will get on with his life, and you'll get on with yours. Archie…" She rolled his name around on her lips and smiled. Maybe she'd stay in England after the war. They would certainly need the help.

A Doctor in the House

Chapter Ten

Archie slapped his book closed and tossed it on the end table. Enough sitting. Drumming chilled fingers on his thigh, he stared out the window. The overcast sky held swollen, pewter-colored clouds. Might he risk a walk before they dumped their watery contents?

He'd be drenched before he left the steps. Sighing, he jumped up from the chair and began to pace. Ten days had passed since his fumbled apology to Emma. He'd avoided the manor to give her space, but he missed seeing the men and doing his bit by visiting them. Perhaps it was time to end his self-imposed exile.

Lord, what would You have me do? I don't want to offend her by showing up unwanted, but it's not right to have conflict between believers. Should I give it another go?

The acrid smell of smoke pricked his nose. Archie lifted his head and sniffed. Definitely an odor of burning wood hung in the air. Jogging from the room, he hurried to the parlor to check the fireplace. Set but unlit. He raced to the upstairs sitting room. Nothing in the hearth.

Was he imagining things?

He descended the stairs and grabbed his coat from the rack. Perhaps he should check the perimeter of the cottage.

Pounding rumbled the front door, and he jerked his head toward the sound. "Sir! Are you in there, Sir Heron?"

Archie yanked open the door. One of the groundskeepers huddled outside, with his sweaty hair spiked in all directions, and his pale face full of terror. A brown, saddled plow horse waited in the driveway.

"What's wrong?"

"It's the big house, sir. There's a fire. The orderlies have started a bucket brigade, but they need more help. The flames are spreading, and we need to get the lads out. Dr. O'Sullivan asked for every available hand. I'm off to Stillwell Farm and Newbury Manor."

"Go!" Archie gestured to the horse before shoving his arms into his coat and sprinting toward his ancestral home. Lungs heaving, he strained to see the majestic building through the trees. Coal-black wisps curled above the branches, and his chest tightened.

Lord, save them! Don't let the lads survive the war only to die in a fire.

Men and women streamed out the front door, some leading the ambulatory patients and others carrying stretchers with men unable to fend for themselves. A line of groundskeepers passed buckets, barrels, and an assortment of containers filled with water from the small pond to a large man at the open kitchen window where smoke spewed. Another group wrestled a hose from the hand-pump to the manor while one of the stable lads cranked the handle up and down.

Searching the mob, Archie looked for Emma's ginger-colored hair and white-jacketed frame. Nurse Milford stood in the driveway directing the chaos, but the feisty doctor was nowhere to be seen.

Was she still inside? Archie's heart skittered. He rushed to the head nurse. "Nurse Milford, where is Emma, er, Dr. O'Sullivan?"

"The last time I saw her she was coordinating efforts upstairs to get everyone out."

His pulse sped up. "What is she thinking? She must leave the house immediately."

"You try telling her that." She raised an eyebrow before turning to a passing orderly. "Take Sir Heron upstairs. Find Dr. O'Sullivan, then report back to me."

"Yes, ma'am." The burly, young man trotted toward the house, Archie close on his heels. They entered the open door and galloped up the steps. Sooty fog filled the corridor, and Archie's eyes teared up. Blinking away the liquid, he bumped against the wall. Men emerged through the smog guiding coughing patients.

"Emma!" Archie waved his arm to dispel the smoke. "Dr. O'Sullivan, where are you?"

The orderly disappeared through a doorway. "Sir Heron, in here!" His disembodied voice was muffled and distant.

Archie entered the ward. Emma stood near the open window, a clipboard in one hand and pencil in the other. What little smoke was in the room wafted above their heads. Three of the beds still held patients sitting on the edge of their mattresses.

He blew out a deep breath. She was safe. For now.

Meeting her eyes, he strode to her side. He grabbed her arm and tugged her toward the door. "You need to leave the house."

She wrenched herself from his grasp, and her face darkened. "What do you think you're doing? I must see to the men. They are my responsibility."

"You have people to take care of these chaps. It's not safe for you to stay here." He reached for her then dropped his hand. "Please. Follow me."

Shaking her head, she frowned. "I'm not leaving this house until every person is accounted for." Orderlies moved the last two patients from the room, and she made tick marks on her paper. "If you'd like to continue this argument, come with me. Otherwise, you might want to think about helping to put out the fire. After all, this is your home. I happen to know it means a lot to you."

Emma pushed past him and marched to the hall. He scrambled to keep up with her as they made their way to the last, dormitory-style room. The smoke had not reached this ward yet. She pointed to the closest bed. "I may be a woman, but I am also an Army officer and don't need to be rescued by some man with misplaced intentions or a guilty conscience or whatever reason sent you here. Now, make yourself useful and get this patient outside. We can argue about your misogynist attitudes once everyone is safe and the fire has been extinguished."

Archie swallowed, and his dry throat protested. After a long moment, he gave her a curt nod. "Fine, but I'll be back for the remaining lads." *Lord, don't let anything happen to her.*

Wrapping his arm around the man's shoulder, Archie led him through the smoky corridor, down the stairs, and out of the house. Once outside, he took the man to one of the nurses before dashing back inside.

As he reached the top of the stairs, a crash sounded from deep within the house. Emma! He made his way to the ward where he'd left her.

Empty. Where is she? "Emma!" Panting, he ducked in and out of each room. All were vacant. His shoes beat a steady rhythm as he descended the stairs. "Emma!"

"Behind that door, sir." A lanky orderly appeared, his normal crisp uniform dingy with grime and soot. "Follow me. We're going to get her out through the back."

"What happened?"

"She was making one last sweep through the house, and one of the ceiling beams gave way above the kitchen. That's where the fire started. Anyway, the falling beam trapped her in the dining room."

Archie's heart clenched. Was she hurt? Afraid?

The pair rushed out the door and circled the house. Rudy draped a blanket over the jagged edge of the window sill and reached into the house. A slim hand grasped his meaty arm, then Emma's head poked through the opening. Her bun had come undone, and strawberry tresses tumbled down her back. A large scratch marred one check, dirt covered the other.

Knees buckling, Archie nearly pitched forward. She seemed unharmed. *Thank You, Lord.* He clenched his hands together and fought the desire to help her climb from the house. She'd made it clear she wanted no part of his rescue attempts.

Moments later, she was standing on the grass checking her clipboard. She had saved her clipboard? He shook his head and grinned. She was tenacious.

He continued to watch her, and she must have felt his gaze because she looked in his direction. Flushing, she ducked her head and brushed at the wrinkles in her skirt.

Archie's stomach fluttered and, before he could change his mind, he darted across the remaining expanse toward Emma. As he swept her into his arms and pressed his lips on hers, the skies opened and deluged them with buckets of water. Her lips stiffened then warmed under his.

Chapter Eleven

Swollen raindrops battered the windows, and thunder rolled overhead as Emma plunked buckets around the ballroom-ward floor to catch the falling drips. The storm was a mixed blessing. Dousing yesterday's flames relieved the men of their back-breaking work and saved the beautiful manor, but the driving rain had been infiltrating the house through the leaky roof since late last night. Her head throbbed, and the steady plink-plink-plink into the pails was a slow form of torture. Fortunately, the patients didn't seem to mind.

Did the government know the home's poor state of repair when they requisitioned it? Why had Archie let the house get this bad? Surely, he was wealthy enough to fix it.

Emma froze, kettle in hand. Did he have the money? Perhaps his family been affected by England's Great Slump which resulted from her own country's Depression. When she saw the majestic home and discovered his title, she assumed he had the riches to accompany them. Perhaps she was wrong.

Footsteps sounded, and Archie entered the room juggling two casks and a barrel. His face was flushed, and his clothing askew. Her heart skipped a beat. His disheveled appearance made him look more handsome than usual. How was that possible?

He grimaced and set his load on the ground.

Was he unhappy to see her? They hadn't discussed yesterday's kiss. The rain pelting them from above had brought them to their senses, and they had dealt with the aftermath of the fire while studiously avoiding each other. Patients had been transported to the other four cottages on the premises, and two of the orderlies had driven to Liverpool to beg for medical supplies from hospitals and doctors' offices. Emma had finally fallen asleep propped on a couch in one of the houses shortly before the sun rose and slept until lunchtime. Until the fire inspector finished his investigation, the patients would remain in their temporary quarters.

"Emma, I've been searching for you. You look exhausted. Did you manage to get any sleep?"

"A bit. But there's so much to be done."

He strode toward her then halted, an uncertain smile on his face. "You mustn't wear yourself out."

"I cannot expect my staff to do all the work." She crossed her arms. "What kind of leader would I be if I directed activities from afar?"

"A sensible one." He closed the distance between them. With a gentle touch, he tucked an errant strand of hair behind her ear. "We need to talk, don't you think?"

Her scalp tingled, and she took a step back. "There's still work to be done. I think it's best that we focus on the task at hand."

His face fell, his smile faltering. "If I offended you…"

"That's not it. There's nothing to discuss." Emma waved her hand back and forth between them. "A relationship between us cannot work. We're from two very different worlds. I'm an American, a military doctor. You're a rich, British Lord. A bit incongruous, yes?" She swallowed past the lump in her throat. "Besides, until yesterday, I thought you hated me."

He winced. "I'm sorry you had that impression. As much as I wanted to do my bit for the war, I didn't want the condition of the manor to become known, and then a certain intelligent, beautiful, American doctor arrived. My pride was wounded further because I didn't want you to find out how bad it was. As you said, you assumed I was a rich Lord. Nothing could be further from the truth."

"What are you saying?"

"My father, God rest his soul, was a kind, decent man, but he was a terrible manager. He didn't have a head for numbers and was more interested in flowers. Horticulture was his passion. He ignored the house, but designed most of the gardens and did a lot of the work himself alongside his groundskeepers. During The Great War, he allowed most of his tenants to fall behind on their rent. Then a scoundrel cheated him by talking him into a fraudulent investment. The man was caught and jailed, but only after he had wasted away the money. Father died of a heart attack shortly after that, and I've been playing catch-up ever since."

Emma grasped his hands. "And the War Department has been slow in sending you payment for the requisition, hasn't it? So, you are left with a houseful of people to feed with no way to provide for them. How awful for you." She cleared her throat. "I'm sorry I misjudged you. Mother always reminds me that I can't possible understand someone until I've walked a mile in his shoes. She'd be horrified at my attitude toward you."

"Then we won't tell her. Besides, you've had your own struggles." He squeezed her fingers. "Can we start over? I don't know how, but in the rather short time we've known each other, I've come to care about you. A lot. Your passion for healing others, your faith in God, and your beauty, both inside and out, have captured my heart. I won't be filing my report. In fact, I'll contact General Winn to let him know what a brilliant job you're doing."

She pulled away and wrapped her arms around her middle. "How can you say you having feelings for me? We've only known each other a few weeks. I'm willing to start over, but we can never be more than friends."

"It's been eleven weeks."

"What?"

"We met eleven weeks ago, today."

"That's my point, we barely know each other."

Archie sighed. "My parents knew each other exactly one month when my father proposed to my mother. They were married for twenty-five years."

"Times were different then." She nibbled her lower lip then squared her shoulders. "Thank you for offering to speak to General Winn. He's not been supportive of my posting here. Perhaps your words will change his opinion."

"You responded to my kiss, Emma. I know you have feelings for me."

Her face warmed, and she pressed her fingers to her lips. "Archie, I'm going home when the war is over. You can't change my mind." What was wrong with her? Before the fire, she had told herself she might stay. Now, Archie had declared his feelings, and she was running for the hills. *Lord, help me. I'm so confused.*

Chapter Twelve

The fire inspector had given his blessing to enter the house, and within hours Archie stood in the entranceway directing the workers' activities. Did he merit such help from people he had ignored over the years?

Booted feet clomped across the wooden floors, and the cacophony of men's voices filled the manor as dozens of villagers cleared away damaged items. Women of all ages entered the house bearing food, sheets and blankets, towels, and cleaning supplies. Laughter punctuated their endeavors making the arduous task seem like a lawn party.

"Sir Heron, a bit of a hoo-ha going on here, wouldn't you say?" Smiling, the vicar waved as he threaded his way through the piles of charred wooden trimmings and furniture. He entered the house and extended his hand. "How are you holding up, old man?"

Archie shook the man's hand then gestured to the chaos. "Overwhelmed. Grateful. Surprised."

"Why are you surprised? You and your family mean a lot to these folks. They do for each other. Why wouldn't they do for you?"

"Vicar Babcock, my father was certainly beloved, but I've barely acknowledged them since my return."

"Doesn't matter. They know you've been through a lot--your injury, the loss of your wife, mum, and brothers. This war has taken its toll on all the families here and reaching out helps them deal with their grief." He clapped his hand on Archie's shoulder. "Today would be a perfect time to get reacquainted with your neighbors. God can make something good of this ordeal."

"My head knows that, but my heart doesn't agree. He's allowed worldwide death and devastation at the hands of a madman. My brothers died in vain." Archie's voice caught, and he swallowed the lump that had formed in his throat.

"Walk with me."

"What?"

"The men have things well in hand here. Let's enjoy the sunshine God sent."

"All right." Archie followed the vicar as he ambled out of the manor.

"Paul told the Thessalonians to 'Rejoice evermore,' and 'In everything give thanks for this is the will of God in Christ Jesus concerning you.' A tough pill to swallow, yes? The Greek words are in the imperative form. A fancy way of saying this is a commandment from God. He is a God of joy and wants us to be joyful. Not *for* our circumstances, but *amongst* them. Christian joy is a feeling on top of the fact that God is in control." The vicar winked. "Have you pushed Him out of the driver's seat?"

Archie let out a shaky breath. "Without a doubt."

"It's not too late to seek His forgiveness, lad. He's waiting with open arms to welcome you back to the fold and to take away your hurt and despair. You may never know why God chose to allow your brothers to die in battle, but they were Christians and are now in heaven with Him. There is a purpose for everything God does, and He can use terrible things that happen for our good."

Vicar Babcock squeezed Archie's shoulder. "Our human selves can't see the wider canvas, so we get discouraged and distraught, but He will give us peace if we ask for it."

"You're a wise man, Vicar. Thank you for coming to see me."

The vicar waved his hand in a dismissive gesture. "I'm only God's messenger, lad. These are His words. And those wonderful people clearing out your house are part of His provision for you. He is taking care of you through the kind deeds of others."

"I don't deserve His goodness."

"None of us does, lad, but it gives Him great pleasure to grant us the desires of our hearts." Vicar Babcock grinned. "And speaking of the heart, I hear there is a lovely, American doctor in charge. You must be enjoying that."

Archie looked away.

The vicar chuckled. "I'd heard you were moonstruck. Seems to be true."

"She won't have me…says she returning to America after the

war."

"Not to make light of the situation, but this war has a long way to go before it's won. You have time to change her mind. You're a charming young man, and if you feel God has sent her to you, He's on your side. Pray about it. Pray *for* her." He poked Archie with his elbow. "I've got a good feeling about this."

Warmth filled Archie, and he gaped at the man. *Is that You, God? What are You saying?*

Chapter Thirteen

Rifling through the stacks of paper on her desk, Emma blew out a sigh. Reports, packing slips, purchase orders, and receipts all served to grease the wheels of bureaucracy, but they left little time for practicing medicine. She hadn't examined a patient since before the fire. Gwen had offered to take over some of the more mundane administration. Perhaps it was time to let her.

The faint sound of a piano filtered into the office, followed by men's voices rumbling a discordant version of *Hark, The Herald Angels Sing*. Ten days until Christmas, and despite being far from home, the nurses and orderlies did a wonderful job of creating a festive atmosphere for the wounded and ill.

Her heart tugged, and she glanced at the watch pinned to her bodice. The six-hour time difference between England and Maryland meant her parents would be sitting in the kitchen working *The Baltimore Sun's* crossword while enjoying their breakfast. Mother was crazy about the holidays, but had she bothered to put up a tree this year?

Rubbing her aching forehead, Emma sniffled. A letter to them was in order. She hadn't written in weeks. They would be worried.

Raucous laughter barreled through the house, and Emma smiled.

The frivolity was just what she needed to chase away her blues. She rose and left the office, closing the door with a firm click. The music began again, and she increased her pace.

She entered the east parlor and stopped, her eyes wide at the gaiety. Some sort of pine tree stood in the far corner covered with strings of popcorn, red bows, and tongue depressors glued in various shaped ornaments. Metal glinted among the boughs. Emma squinted and tilted her head. Were those medical instruments hanging from the branches? She giggled to herself. General Winn would have something to say about that.

Pine wreaths hung at each window, and a mammoth kissing ball made of holly dangled from the chandelier. Some industrious soul seemed to have collected every crimson-colored article of clothing on the grounds. Tied together in unorthodox garlands, they hung from every horizontal surface.

Emma smiled at Gwen as she approached. "You and the nurses have outdone yourselves with decorations, although I hope you left me some equipment."

"A few bits, and we can always borrow from the tree and give the item a good sterilization." Gwen nudged Emma's shoulder. "Nice to have you join us. I was getting ready to send Archie up for you. You've done enough work for today."

"The noise made it difficult to concentrate."

"Ha. I don't think so. You knew you were missing out."

The piano music quit, and the men's applause filled the room. Archie grinned and made an exaggerated show of joining his hands and cracking his knuckles. He glanced at Emma and winked before turning his attention back to the keys.

Her pulse quickened, and she ducked her head.

Gwen chuckled and leaned closer. "He's swell, isn't he? A real hotsy-totsy."

Emma swatted Gwen's arm. "Shh! Someone will hear you."

"Not likely. They're all focused on our very own Stan Kenton. Besides, everyone has seen the two of you making eyes at each other."

"Nonsense. Granted, we've put aside our differences, but we've agreed that friendship is as far as it goes."

"Right. Just friends. That's why he spends every day in the manor and watches you when he thinks no one is looking. And that's why you blush and stammer when he's around." She shook her head. "Sorry, sister, that's more than friendship, and you know it."

"Once this war is over and done with, we'll go our separate ways. I'll head back to the States." Her hands trembled, and she stuffed them in her pockets.

"It doesn't have to be like that. The English will need our help long after the hostilities end. They're a stalwart people, but they've lost so many in the fray. I plan to stay, and I know a certain British gentlemen who would be thrilled if you remained, too."

Emma studied her feet, and her stomach quivered. Archie had

declared his feelings for her, and she had scoffed, not believing they were real because of the short time they'd known each other. He must have been hurt by her insensitivity, yet he had shown no sign of it. In fact, he had continued to tease her in private and treat her with respect in public.

She froze, her heart pounding. Was Gwen right? Did he care for Emma with a forever kind of love? Did she feel the same way, or was this nothing more than wartime infatuation?

Raising her head, she peeked in the direction of the piano. Archie banged away at the keys, but his eyes were riveted on her. A tingling sensation swept over Emma's body, and she rubbed at her arms. Her breath caught.

This was definitely more than friendship.

Chapter Fourteen

Swirling snowflakes dampened Archie's wool coat in the crisp air. The fingernail-like sliver of the moon played hide and seek among the clouds as he walked from the darkened cottage to the blacked-out manor. Four inches of white, fluffy powder had already accumulated in the short time since the storm began. Perhaps a night better spent finishing *Great Expectations* by the fire, but missing the Christmas Eve service was not an option.

Humming *Joy to the World,* he held out his hand to catch the falling snow, then squinted at his glove. Impossible to see the melting flakes. He stuffed his fisted hands into the pockets of his coat and increased his stride.

"No dawdling, Heron. Emma promised to sit with you, and you don't want to keep her waiting." Archie's voice sent puffs of vapor out of his mouth, and he grinned. Flexing his lips, he tried to produce smoke-rings with no success. "Get a grip, old man. You're acting like a schoolboy."

The hulking shape of the house loomed in the darkness. Following the shoveled lane one of the groundskeepers must have cleared, Archie made his way to the front door. He shook the wetness from his shoulders and slipped inside. Closing the door behind him, he stood for a moment in the dimly lit entrance.

Tony appeared on silent feet. Dressed in dark slacks and a light blue shirt with his hair slicked down, he looked nothing like the daytime, uniformed orderly. "Take your coat, Sir Heron?"

Archie nodded and shrugged out of his soggy overcoat. "Thank you, Tony. You're looking dapper tonight."

"Thank you, sir."

"Archie. I've told you lads to call me Archie." Stamping his booted feet to shed the water from them, he patted Tony's shoulder and then hurried down the corridor toward the east parlor. The buzz of conversation punctuated by laughter greeted him as he stepped into the candle-lit room.

Letting the voices wash over him, Archie hesitated. As he searched the room for Emma, a few of the men lifted their hands in greeting, and he waved in return. Where was she? He pulled out his pocket watch and popped it open. Twenty minutes before the service was scheduled to start. Was she getting dressed or immersed in paperwork and oblivious to the time?

"She'll be here, Archie." The head nurse appeared at his elbow, an impish grin on her face. "I just pried her out of the office and sent her upstairs. She doesn't want to work on Christmas Day, so she was finishing up her weekly report for General Winn. No rest for the weary, you know."

"She works too hard."

"That she does, but the staff has insisted the good doctor take tomorrow off. They've promised to handle everything, and unless we're sent additional casualties, it should be a quiet day." Gwen waggled her eyebrows. "Perhaps the two of you can spend some time together."

Archie's pulse skittered, and he licked his dry lips. "Perhaps."

Shaking her head, Gwen sighed. "You're as bad as Emma. Both of you besotted with one another, yet denying there's anything more than friendship. Good grief, Archie, you're hopeless, and you're going to lose out if you don't do something." She pointed to three empty chairs in the front row. "I'll be over there. The other two seats are for you and Emma. Don't tarry, I'm sure the vicar has a humdinger of a sermon planned."

She wove her way through the crowd, and Archie turned toward the door. Moments later, Emma appeared, and his breath caught. Tortoiseshell combs held her glistening hair back on either side of her head, and waves of ginger-colored strands tumbled past her shoulders. Wearing an emerald-green velvet dress, she clutched a small Bible in her hands. Black peep-toe shoes covered her feet.

"You are a vision of loveliness, Emma." He held out his arm. "May I escort you to our seats? Gwen has saved us a pair next to her."

Emma's face flushed, and she tucked her hand into the crook of his elbow. Warmth permeated his sleeve, and he faltered. Did she have any idea how she affected him?

"God sent His Son to give us *abundant* life, not a mediocre life. And the way to have an abundant life is to be living in His will, not our own. Too often we get caught up in the tasks of day-to-day living and forget about the big picture. He will lead us into an exciting future, a future we've never considered. What is He telling you, dear ones? Are you avoiding God's plans for you out of fear?"

Vicar Babcock hugged his arms to himself and gave an exaggerated shudder. "The future can be scary if we try to fend for ourselves, but with God by our side, we can stride through life with confidence. God sent His Son to give us abundant life. Now what is He telling you, dear ones?"

Archie blinked. *Are You talking to me, Father? First Gwen tells me to speak out, and now the vicar seems to be speaking directly to me. Do Your plans for me include Emma?* He peeked at her through lowered lids. Her gaze was fixed on the speaker, and she seemed…peaceful. Had she come to some sort of decision? Did it include him?

Chapter Fifteen

Emma tugged her scarf closer around her neck and huddled into her coat as she tramped through the field. Sometime during the night, the storm subsided, blanketing the grassy expanse with nearly eight inches of heavy, wet snow. Her ears and nose tingled in the cold, and she wiggled her toes inside the borrowed Wellies to keep her circulation moving.

She had awakened early, her thoughts whirling on last night's sermon. After waiting for the sun to crest the horizon, she dressed quickly and left the manor. It seemed appropriate to be alone with God on the birthday of His Son.

Streaks of pink and purple filled the sky. A lone bird swooped back and forth above her head, apparently enjoying his own solitude. A red deer stag bellowed in the distance.

A red deer. Did Archie hear the animal's cry? How much things had changed since the hunting incident.

Archie's face filled her mind, and she wrapped her arms around her middle against the fluttering in her stomach. Would he be at the Christmas feast? He had again used his connections-this time to secure several pheasant for the meal. Surely he would join in the celebration. Her heart picked up speed, and she stretched out her arms, twirling as best as the cumbersome boots would let her.

She stopped and looked at the robin's egg blue heavens. "I do care about him, Father. More than I realized. More than I thought possible. He's kind and gentle, and a follower of You." Her face heated. "And he's handsome too. What am I supposed to do?"

The clouds parted, and the suns ray sparkled and glowed.

"Reminding me of Your sovereignty, are You?" Emma smiled and shielded her eyes from the glare. "What a beautiful morning, Lord. Thank You for Your creation and for the blessings You continue to shower on me. You've given me so many of the desires of my heart that I don't deserve. Thank You for sending Jesus to save me. Forgive me for running ahead of You. Help me to wait on You and to enjoy each day in Your presence." As she spoke, her breath froze in smoke-like wisps.

Warmth filled her, and Emma's lips curved in a smile. She giggled and dropped to the ground. Flat on her back, she moved her arms up and down and her legs side to side. Climbing to her feet, she shook the snow off her clothes and grinned. "A perfect snow angel."

A shout sounded, and she turned. In the distance, Archie lifted his hand in greeting. She waved back before pressing a hand against her chest where her heart throbbed. "Steady, girl."

Moments later he was close enough to speak. "Happy Christmas, Emma. You're up and out early."

She dipped her head. "Merry Christmas. I could say the same about you."

Archie smiled. "I was hoping to sneak into the house to leave you a gift, but couldn't resist joining you." He gestured to her art work. "You make a lovely snow angel."

"Years of practice. Maryland winters are not long, but we do get snow, and I learned early on how to make an angel." She bent and packed the snow into a sphere. "But I'm really good at this!" She whipped the snowball at Archie, and it exploded against the front of his coat.

Laughing, she raised her arms and danced a victory jig.

His eyes widened. Brushing off the ice crystals, he chuckled. "So, that's how it's going to be." He scooped up a handful of snow and flung it at her. Missing her, the ball landed with a muffled thud.

"You throw like a girl!" Emma guffawed then pelted him with balls. "I warned you."

He ran toward her, and she dropped her weapons, shrieking as she stumbled through the drifts. Floundering, she fell in a heap. He pulled her to her feet then slung her over his shoulder. Breathless, she pummeled his back with her fists. "Put me down."

"Not yet." Archie marched to the house and set her down near the snow-covered debris from the fire. Turning her toward him, he grasped her gloved hands. She shivered at his touch, and her toes curled inside her boots.

"Emma, I need you. You said it yourself, it's only been a few weeks since we met, but I feel as if I've known you all of my life. You fill a part of me I thought would stay empty forever. I have very little to offer you, darling." He jerked his head toward the pile. "A title, a stack of rubbish, and quite a bit of debt. But I've a keen mind, and I can seek a job in Liverpool to provide for you. Or if you wanted to go home when the war is over, I will do whatever it takes to join you there. I love you, no matter where we live." He dropped to one knee and looked up at her. "Would you do me the honor of becoming my wife?"

Tears filled Emma's eyes, and her heart pounded. Archie didn't just care for her. He loved her. She swiped the moisture from her face and nodded.

"You will? Oh, sweetheart, you've made me the happiest man on earth." He leapt to his feet and swept her into his arms. Lowering his head, he pressed his lips on hers.

Her breath mingling with his, Emma wrapped her arms around Archie's neck. Their kiss deepened, and she sighed. Moments later, she pulled away and gazed into his eyes. "There's no reason for me to return to the States. I'm happy to stay in England. Home is wherever you are."

The End

Acknowledgments

Although writing a book is a solitary task, it is not a solitary journey. There have been many who have helped and encouraged me along the way.

My parents, Richard and Jean Shenton, who presented me with my first writing tablet and encouraged me to capture my imagination with words. Thanks, Mom and Dad!

Scribes212 – my ACFW online critique group: Valerie Goree, Marcia Lahti, and the late Loretta Boyett (passed on to Glory, but never forgotten). Without your input, my writing would not be nearly as effective.

Eva Marie Everson – my mentor/instructor with Christian Writers' Guild. You took a timid, untrained student and turned her into a writer. Many thanks!

SincNE, and the folks who coordinate the Crimebake Writing Conference. I have attended many writing conferences, but without a doubt, Crimebake is one of the best. The workshops, seminars, panels, critiques, and every tiny aspect are well-executed, professional, and educational.

Special thanks to Hank Phillippi Ryan, Halle Ephron, and Roberta Isleib for your encouragement and spot-on critiques of my work.

Thanks to my Book Brigade who provide information, encouragement, and support.

Paula Proofreader (https://paulaproofreader.wixsite.com/home): I'm so glad I found you! My work is cleaner because of your eagle eye. Any mistakes are completely mine.

A heartfelt thank you to my brothers, Jack Shenton and Douglas Shenton, and my sister, Susan Shenton Greger for being enthusiastic cheerleaders during my writing journey. Your support means more than you'll know.

My husband, Wes, deserves special kudos for understanding my need to write. Thank you for creating my writing room – it's perfect, and I'm thankful for it every day. Thank you for your willingness to accept a house that's a bit cluttered, laundry that's not always done, and meals on the go. I love you.

And finally, to God be the glory. I thank Him for giving me the gift of writing and the inspiration to tell stories that shine the light on His goodness and mercy.

Want more romance? Read on for the first chapter of *Spies & Sweethearts, Sisters in Service, book 1.*

Chapter One

Just because she was the eldest, did Cora have to criticize Emily's every decision? She was a high school French teacher, not a schoolgirl. Shaking her head, Emily climbed on the bike and pedaled away from the house. She'd exhausted her gas rations for the week, so using the car was out. Fortunately, the library wasn't far. She could finish preparing the end-of-year exams there.

Two of her students were already gone. Days after they turned eighteen, the boys talked the principal into letting them graduate early in order to enlist. Her heart constricted. Now, both were in training with the army air force and would soon be on their way overseas to fight the Germans. They spoke French impeccably, a skill better used in the ambassador ranks rather than on an airplane.

The warm air stroked Emily's cheeks as she rode. Squinting against the sun's glare, she huffed out a breath. At least the boys were doing something for the war effort. Her service with the American Women's Voluntary Services as a plane spotter and messenger wasn't exactly going to turn the tide against the Axis powers. Surely, there was something more she could do.

She braked in front of the sandstone building and wheeled her bike into an empty spot in one of the racks near the entrance of Trafalgar Public Library. A Carnegie library, it housed several hundred books thanks to the Scottish-American philanthropist. What would he think of the war?

"Emily!"

A broad grin on her face, Joan Boyer hurried toward Emily. Her floral dress danced around her leg, and her ponytail flounced. "Your mom said I'd find you here." Her smile faltered. "Are you okay? You look terrible."

"Gee, thanks. Glad I can count on you for support."

"What?"

Emily finger-combed her hair. "I'm sorry. I had another argument with Cora. Just because she's already been married and widowed, she thinks she knows what's good for everyone."

Joan linked her arm through Emily's. "Let's grab a seat in the memorial garden. You can tell me everything."

They sauntered to the wooden bench sheltered by a large, weeping cherry tree and surrounded by black-eyed Susans, and a rainbow of coneflowers and petunias nodding in the breeze.

"All right. What gives? You've been annoyed with Cora in the past, but you seem especially angry today."

"I am." Emily slumped against the seat. "True or not, it feels like neither she nor Doris take me seriously because I'm the youngest. That all I'm good enough for is teaching a bunch of kids. A few days ago, Cora commented that plane spotting night duty must be interfering with my job, and she didn't understand why I was still volunteering. Like I can't juggle multiple responsibilities. I'm almost twenty-six years old. I'm quite capable."

"Maybe she worries about you."

"Perhaps, but it doesn't seem like concern. It feels like criticism of my life." Emily fisted her hands. "This morning, I got a letter telling me I've been accepted into a new government program. I leave for training the day after school is out. She overheard me telling Mom about the job and quizzed me about it. When I told her I couldn't share specifics, she rolled her eyes and asked what the government needed with a schoolteacher."

"That's awful." Joan squeezed Emily's shoulder.

"The worst of it is that once she got started down that road, Mom followed…said I should rethink the opportunity…that I have a perfectly good job here at home, and my volunteer work is sufficient." She frowned. "Then Mom said I'm being selfish to go off on my own. It's bad enough I'm still living at home at my age, but for them to try to dictate my decisions is too much."

"What are you going to do?"

"Send a telegram accepting the position. I've got to live my own life no matter what they say." She blinked away tears forming in her eyes. "Do you think I'm being self-centered by going?"

"Absolutely not. Your parents are in perfect health, and Cora is living here, too. She can take care of any needs they might have." Joan leaned forward. "You really can't say much about the job? Not even a little?"

The tightness in Emily's chest eased, and she chuckled. "You always could make me feel better. I'm sorry for not telling you I applied, but I was skeptical I'd get selected. You should have seen the crowd. Anyway, I don't know a lot about the job. There is a new governmental department, and it needs people who are bilingual. The exam contained lots of translation exercises, especially with regard to colloquialisms and dialect for different regions in France and French-speaking countries."

"Now you know how your students feel."

"Absolutely, but that doesn't mean I'm going to go easy on them for the final." Emily rubbed her damp palms on her skirt. "I can't believe this will be my last year of teaching for a while…maybe forever. I'm a bit nervous about notifying the principal about leaving. The factories pay much higher than the schools, so Medford has had a lot of resignations. The school may have to combine classes next year."

"This war won't last forever. In fact, some say it will be over by Christmas. Surely you'll be back."

Emily shook her head. "I don't want to be a naysayer, but I doubt the war will be over by the end of the year. I think we're in this for the long haul."

"Can you at least tell me where you're going? I could come visit."

"I've forgotten the address, somewhere in Washington, DC, but that's not my final stop. I'll be transported with other new employees to the training facility where I'll stay for three months. I won't be able to send or receive letters while I'm there. And definitely no visitors."

Joan bolted upright. "That sounds intriguing, very secretive. If you're lucky, there will be a few dreamboats in the class."

"Romance is the last thing I need, Joan. Besides, guys our age are in the defense industry or armed forces. There won't be anyone to fall in love with."

Gerard Lucas resisted the urge to run a finger around the collar of his dress uniform to loosen the stifling piece of clothing. What he wouldn't give to be in a flannel shirt and pair of overalls. Out in the field, wind ruffling his hair, and acres of crops flourishing in the sunshine. Perhaps a beautiful woman by his side. And—

"Lieutenant Lucas, are you listening to me?"

Gerard wrenched his thoughts back to the present and snapped his heels together. "Sir, yes, sir."

"Insulting and then arguing with a higher ranking officer in front of his men and the local Brits is a serious offense. The only things keeping you out of the brig or a dishonorable discharge are this war and the fact you didn't take a poke at him. The country needs all the men we can get." Major Albert shook his head. "You're a bright guy, one who should be climbing the ranks rather than getting demoted every three months. You are lucky Major Quigley had you reduced to private."

"Sir, he didn't know what he was talking about—"

"I did not give you permission to speak, and therein lies your problem. Failure to respect the chain of command. You are to obey orders without question and to show respect to those ranked above you. You're arrogant and argumentative. More than a few officers have made that observation. Not a good combination, Lucas." The major dropped into the chair behind his desk. "You need to apologize to Major Quigley. In public. At the pub where the incident occurred."

"Yes, sir."

"Excellent. Now, the good news for everyone is that you are being transferred to an intelligence unit based out of Washington, DC. Apparently, your penchant for getting into trouble is a desirable trait to them."

Gerard's heart sped up. There'd been stories about guerrilla warfare and espionage, but he figured the information was rumor, like most of what he heard in between training exercises. Was he finally going to see the war up close? Or rather, behind the scenes?

Major Albert tossed him a set of papers then gestured to the vacant chair. "At ease, Soldier."

Dropping into the seat, Gerard tugged at his collar and sighed. The material still scratched his skin and threatened to suffocate him. He picked his orders and scanned the instructions. He had two days to prepare. To wait and wonder what was in store for him.

"As you can see, you leave the day after tomorrow. Unless you run into a hitch, you'll report for duty on Saturday. Try not to mess this up. It may be your last chance to remain a free man."

"Permission to speak candidly, sir?"

"I'd expect nothing less, Lucas."

"Why me?"

"Why you, what?"

"You must have recommended me, sir. Otherwise, how would they know about me?" Gerard studied the major. "So why did you put my name forward for consideration?"

"It appears I haven't underestimated your abilities. You're right. I did recommend you." Major Albert smirked. "This new department…they're calling it the Office of Strategic Services…a positively bureaucratic label, if you ask me, but maybe that's what they want everyone to think. Personally, from the bits and pieces I've been able to glean, it's more like the department of dirty tricks. Anyway, that sounded like something you'd be suited for. You know, swimming against the tide."

"I appreciate your faith in me, sir. I won't let you down."

"It's not me I'm worried about. Don't let yourself down, Lucas. You've got to come to terms with whatever's eating you. Yes, you don't suffer fools, and that's fine, but it's more than that. You're carting around a lot of anger. Maybe you know why. Maybe you don't. Either way, you need to channel those feelings or jettison them, because if you don't, you'll get yourself killed. Understood?"

"Yes, sir."

Major Albert steepled his fingers. "Quigley wanted to bring you up on charges, put you through a court-martial, but I talked him out of it."

"Thank you, sir."

"I'm not looking for gratitude. I'm telling you because this is your last chance. Not everyone is willing to accept your shenanigans. And despite the roguish nature of your new assignment, there will be some sort of hierarchy. Adhere to it, or you may not survive this war." He rose and extended his hand. "Good luck, son, and Godspeed."

They shook hands. Gerard put on his peaked wool cap, saluted, then pivoted and hurried from the room, a grin tugging at his lips. Finally, a chance to avenge his brother's death in the Atlantic at the hands of a German submarine wolfpack.

Other Titles
Romance

Love at First Flight

Love's Harvest, Wartime Brides, Book 1

Love's Rescue, Wartime Brides, Book 2

Love's Belief, Wartime Brides, Book 3

Love's Allegiance, Wartime Brides, Book 4

Love Found in Sherwood Forest

A Love Not Forgotten

On the Rails

Spies & Sweethearts, Sisters in Service, Book 1

The Mechanic & the MD, Sisters in Service, Book 2

The Widow & the War Correspondent, Sisters in Service, Book 3

Dinah's Dilemma (Westward Home & Hearts Mail-Order Brides, 10)

Mystery
Under Fire, Ruth Brown Mystery Series, Book 1

Under Ground, Ruth Brown Mystery Series, Book 2

Under Cover, Ruth Brown Mystery Series, Book 3

Murder of Convenience, Women of Courage, Book 1

Murder at Madison Square Garden, Women of Courage, Book 2

Non-Fiction
WWII Word Find, Volume 1

Biography

Linda Shenton Matchett writes about ordinary people who did extraordinary things in days gone by. She is a volunteer docent and archivist at the Wright Museum of WWII and a trustee for her local public library. Born in Baltimore, Maryland, a stone's throw from Fort McHenry, she has lived in historical places most of her life. Now located in central New Hampshire, Linda's favorite activities include exploring historic sites and immersing herself in the imaginary worlds created by other authors.

Website/blog: http://www.LindaShentonMatchett.com
Facebook: http://www.facebook.com/LindaShentonMatchettAuthor
Pinterest: http://www.pinterest.com/lindasmatchett
Amazon: https://www.amazon.com/Linda-Shenton-Matchett/e/B01DNB54S0
Goodreads: http://www.goodreads.com/author_linda_matchett
Bookbub: http://www.bookbub.com/authors/linda-shenton-matchett